Ten in the Bed

for Felice
J.C.

ISBN-13: 978-0-545-00097-0
ISBN-10: 0-545-00097-1

Copyright © 2006 by Jane Cabrera
All rights reserved. Published by Scholastic Inc., 557 Broadway, New
York, NY 10012, by arrangement with Holiday House, Inc. SCHOLASTIC
and associated logos are trademarks and/or registered trademarks of
Scholastic Inc.

12 11 10 9 8 7 6 5 4 3 2 1   7 8 9 10 11/0

Printed in the U.S.A.   40

This edition first printing, January 2007

Ten in the Bed

Jane Cabrera

SCHOLASTIC INC.
New York   Toronto   London   Auckland   Sydney
Mexico City   New Delhi   Hong Kong   Buenos Aires

Here is the Little One
A tired and sleepy head.
Stretching and yawning
He's ready for bed.

But...

There were **ten** in the bed
And the **Little One** said
"**Move** over, move over."

So they all rolled over
And the **Snorer**
fell out.

9 There were **nine** in the bed
And the **Little One** said
"Move over, move over."

So they all rushed over
And the **Cook** fell out.

There were **eight** in the bed
And the **Little One** said
"Move over, move over."

So they all bounced over
And the **Trumpeter** fell out.

7

There were **Seven** in the bed
And the **Little One** said
"Move over, move over."

So they all groaned over
And the **Doctor**
fell out.

There were six in the bed
And the Little One said
"Move over. move over."

So they all leaped over
And the **Ballerina** fell out.

5

There were **five** in the bed
And the **Little One** said
"Move over, move over."

So they all swayed over
And the **Pirate fell out.**

4

There were **four** in the bed
And the **Little One** said
"**Move over, move over.**"

So they all bowed over
And the **Princess fell out.**

There were
three in the bed
And the **Little One** said
"Move over, move over."

So they all wobbled over
And the **Pilot**
fell out.

3

2

There were **TWO** in the bed
And the **Little One** said
"Move over, move over."
So the Astronaut floated over
And **she fell out.**

There was **one** in the bed
And **everyone** said
"Move over, move over."

So the little one moved over
And he...

Snorer

Cook

Trumpeter

Doctor

Ballerina

...they all danced about!
Then the **Little One** screamed
And he gave a big shout...

"Settle down now,
settle down now!"

Pirate

Pilot

Princess

Astronaut

Little
One

So they all settled down and went to sleep.
There was not a sound, there was not a peep.
Until the Little One said . . .

"Good night!"